The Pear Tree

sparrows chirping

bees bumbling

a spider spinning

a squirrel scuttling

a sleeping ladybird

a slow snail

For Louis and Theo who live next
door to my pear tree – M.H.

With thanks to Nick for patience, cups
of tea and pipe cleaners – B.W.

Author's Note

The pear tree in this book is home to many different animals. Birds, squirrels, ants, bees and butterflies all live amongst the branches, in holes and sheltered places. Every month more animals use the pear tree. Spiders spin their webs between the twigs, beetles crawl in the bark, and wasps devour the pears.

By December many animals have hidden themselves away, and you can't see them very easily. In this book they are not quite so hidden which makes it easier for you to find and count them. On the last two pages of this book the squirrels are sleeping in their nest, so you won't be able to see them.

First published in 1998 by Macmillan Children's Books
a division of Macmillan Publishers Limited
25 Eccleston Place, London SW1W 9NF, and Basingstoke
Associated companies worldwide

ISBN 0 333 73252 9 (HB)
ISBN 0 333 73253 7 (PB)

Text copyright © 1998 Meredith Hooper
Illustrations copyright © 1998 Bee Willey

The right of Meredith Hooper and Bee Willey to be identified as
the author and illustrator of this work has been asserted
by them in accordance with the Copyright Designs and Patents Act 1988.

1 3 5 7 9 8 6 4 2

A CIP catalogue record for this book is available
from the British Library

Printed in Hong Kong

The Pear Tree

An animal counting book

MEREDITH HOOPER

BEE WILLEY

MACMILLAN
CHILDREN'S BOOKS

On the first day of January
My grandpa showed to me
A pigeon in a pear tree.

On the first day of February
My grandma showed to me
Two speckled starlings
And a pigeon in a pear tree.

On the first day of March
My dad showed to me
Three fat bees
Two starlings in a hole
And a pigeon in a pear tree.

On the first day of April
My mum showed to me
Four furry squirrels
Three busy bees
Two starlings bringing moss
And a pigeon in a pear tree.

On the first day of May
My sister showed to me
Five ladybirds
Four squirrels chasing
Three bees finding pollen
Two starlings bringing grubs
And a pigeon in a pear tree.

On the first day of June
My brother showed to me
Six fluttering butterflies
Five ladybirds
Four squirrels leaping
Three bees flying
Two starlings drinking
And a pigeon in a pear tree.

On the first day of July
My dog showed to me
Seven noisy sparrows
Six butterflies swooping
Five ladybirds
Four squirrels running
Three bees working
Two starlings flapping
And a pigeon in a pear tree.

On the first day of August
My auntie showed to me
Eight ants in a line
Seven sparrows chirping
Six butterflies dancing
Five ladybirds
Four squirrels scratching
Three bees bumbling
Two starlings whistling
And a pigeon in a pear tree.

On the first day of September
My mum showed to me
Nine spiders spinning
Eight ants darting
Seven sparrows pecking
Six butterflies basking
Five ladybirds
Four squirrels nibbling
Three bees buzzing
Two starlings perching
And a pigeon in a pear tree.

On the first day of October
My dad showed to me
Ten stripy wasps
Nine spiders catching flies
Eight ants finding food
Seven sparrows eating seeds
Six butterflies gliding
Five ladybirds
Four squirrels hiding nuts
Three bees going home
Two starlings tugging worms
And a pigeon in a pear tree.

On the first day of November
My grandma showed to me
Eleven shiny beetles
Ten wasps creeping slowly
Nine spiders mending webs
Eight black ants
Seven fluffed–up sparrows
Six butterflies resting
Five ladybirds
Four squirrels digging holes
Three bees crawling
Two starlings in the wind
And a pigeon in a pear tree.

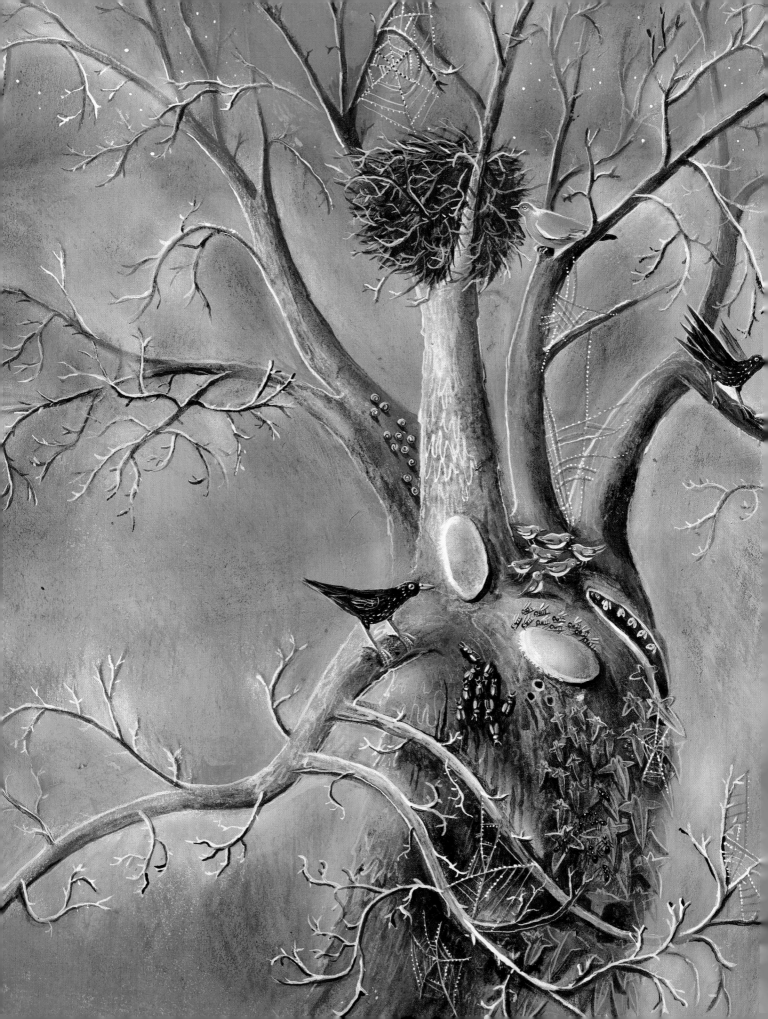

On the first day of December
My grandpa showed to me
Twelve closed–up snails
Eleven beetles in the bark
Ten dried–up wasps
Nine spider webs
Eight ants in the ivy
Seven huddled sparrows
Six sleeping butterflies
Five hidden ladybirds
Four squirrels in their nest
Three holes for bees
Two hungry starlings
And a pigeon in a pear tree.

sparrows chirping

bees bumbling

a spider spinning

a squirrel scuttling

a sleeping ladybird

a slow snail

butterflies swooping

a stripy wasp

a starling whistling

a shining beetle

a pigeon in a pear tree

ants working